WALT DISNEY PRODUCTIONS

presents

ALADDIN and the
Dancing Princess

Random House   🏠   New York

First American Edition. Copyright © 1983 by **The Walt Disney Company.** All rights reserved under International and
Pan-American Copyright Conventions. Published in the United States by Random House, Inc., New York, and simulta-
neously in Canada by Random House of Canada Limited, Toronto. Originally published in Denmark as ALADDIN OG
DEN DANSENDE PRINSESSE by Gutenberghus Gruppen, Copenhagen. ISBN: 0-394-85762-3. Manufactured in the
United States of America   7 8 9 0   B C D E F G H I J K

Book Club Edition

One day Aladdin set out from his palace home.

He was going to visit a friend, the sultan of the desert kingdom.

Aladdin rode in front.

Behind him came a caravan filled with rich gifts for the sultan.

Aladdin rode into the desert.
Suddenly there was a sandstorm!
Aladdin's horse was terrified!

Aladdin's horse
would not lie down
as the camels did.

The horse was so scared
that it ran away.
Aladdin tried to follow,
but he couldn't see.

Soon Aladdin was
lost in the storm.

He tried to reach the shelter of
some palm trees.
But the storm was too much for him.
Aladdin fell to the ground.

When the storm ended, the caravan sadly
made their way to the sultan's palace.
"Welcome!" said the sultan. "But where
is Aladdin?"

"Lost in the storm, Your Majesty,"
said the caravan leader.

"We must find Aladdin!"
cried the sultan.
He called for men
and horses.

In no time they were on their way.

The sultan himself
led the search party
into the desert.

After a while they came to some palm trees.
And there on the ground lay Aladdin!
"Bring water!" cried the sultan.

The water soon made Aladdin better.
Aladdin was very happy to see his friend.
The sultan gave Aladdin a fine new horse,
and off they rode to the palace.

The sultan's daughter, the princess,
served them hot spiced coffee.
Everyone was happy...except
the princess.
She was tired and sad.

Soon the princess said good night.

"What a lovely girl!" said Aladdin.
"But why is she so tired and sad?"

"Oh, I am so worried
about her!" said the sultan.
"Let me show you something."

The sultan called out an order.
A servant brought him a pair of
worn-out slippers.

"Every night the princess wears out a pair
of dancing slippers," said the sultan.
"But she never leaves her room!"

"That is a real mystery," said Aladdin.
"Are you sure she never leaves?"

"She would be seen," said the sultan.
"Come see for yourself."

"The princess sleeps up in
that tower," said the sultan.

Aladdin said, "Let me be the guard tonight."

That night Aladdin hid
outside the princess's room.

At midnight he heard
a loud CRASH!
He peeped through
the keyhole.

The princess was dressed for dancing.
She had knocked over a large vase.
"Thank goodness nobody heard me!"
she said.

Then she pushed
aside a curtain...

and opened
a secret door.

In an instant
the princess was
gone!

Aladdin ran to look over the wall.
Sure enough, there was the princess.
And a handsome prince was waiting for her!

The prince swept
the princess up to
his saddle, and they
quickly rode off
in the moonlight.

Aladdin rubbed
the magic medal that
he wore on a chain
around his neck.
POOF!
The genie of the
medal appeared.

"What is your wish,
O Master?" the genie
asked.
"Take me to
the princess,"
said Aladdin.

And the next thing Aladdin knew...

he was in the ballroom
of a splendid palace.
   And there was the
princess, dancing with
her handsome prince!
   Aladdin hid behind
a palm and watched
them.

The prince and the princess
danced the night away.

Before they knew it, the sun
was rising.

Quickly they ran down
the palace stairs.
One of the princess's
slippers fell off.

Aladdin picked up
the worn-out slipper.

Aladdin watched the couple ride across the desert toward the sultan's palace.

Then he rubbed
his magic medal and
POOF! the genie
appeared.

"Take me to the
princess's room!"
said Aladdin.

And the next thing
he knew...

he was back in the princess's room,
still holding the slipper.

A moment later the princess
limped through the secret door.

She gasped when she saw Aladdin.

"Oh, what will my father say?" cried
the princess. "I want to marry the prince,
but my father thinks I am too young!"

"Let me talk to your father," said Aladdin. "Maybe I can help."

Aladdin told the sultan the whole story.

The sultan was so happy to know the truth that he agreed to the match.

The sultan sent word for the prince
to come.

Aladdin was the guest of honor
at the wedding.

The guests ate and drank and made merry.
And the prince and princess danced for hours.

After the wedding Aladdin said good-bye.
The princess gave him a kiss.
"Thank you for helping me," she said.

The sultan and the prince and princess
all waved good-bye to Aladdin.

"Have a safe journey home!" they called.

The next day Aladdin reached his own palace.
His wife, Princess Minnie, ran out to greet him.

Aladdin couldn't wait to tell her about
the mystery of the dancing princess!